Scardio the Sea Hor

- Hannah Henderson–

Printed and bound in England by www.printondemand-worldwide.com

http://www.fast-print.net/bookshop

Scardio the Sea Horse
Copyright © Hannah Henderson

ISBN: 978-178456-623-4

A catalogue record for this book is available from the British Library

First published 2019 by
FASTPRINT PUBLISHING
Peterborough, England.

This is the story of a beautiful strong Grey stallion called Scardio.

Scardio was born on Lombok Island in Indonesia.

When Scardio was two years old, he was standing with his mother when a big truck pulled up in yard. A man approached Scardio and gently slipped a leather headcollar on him.

Scardio paused for a little, knowing this would be the last time he saw his mother, and with a tear in her eye she said knowingly "my son, you were born to win, never look behind you, keep your head up, ears pricked and focus on what is ahead of you."

With these last words, he was lead away to a new life with new friends and exciting times ahead.

When the truck came to a standstill, the ramp was lowered and Scardio stepped off into an huge brick racing yard, surrounded by tall, beautiful horses with shiny coats and big muscles.

Over the years, Scardio trained hard; he thought of his mother's words and they kept him focused. Time after time, the crowds cheered as he won race after race.

10

5 years passed and Scardio felt his body slow. The years of training had taken its toll and he found it harder to win the races he so desperately wanted to win.

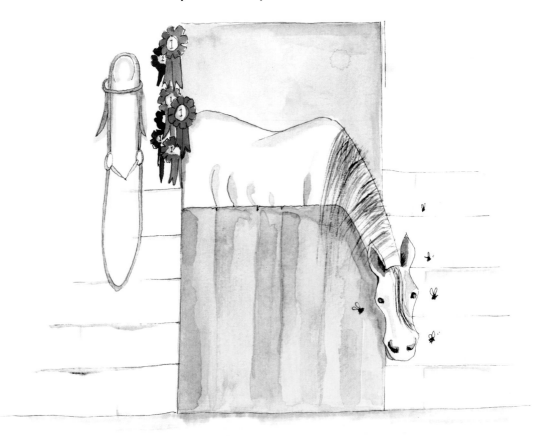

Scardio was sold to a smaller stable yard. The beds were not as clean or comfy, the food did not taste quite so nice, the jockeys were rougher and not as kind as they were once before.

It wasn't long before Scardio noticed the crowds were not chanting his name or cheering him on and he couldn't remember the last time he had won a race.

Time skipped by and Scardio felt his body weaken. One day on the way to a paddock, he caught a glimpse of his reflection in a car window.

He was shocked. It was a mere shell of his original beautiful strong self, which had glistened with lean muscles and shone in the sunshine. Instead, all Scardio saw was a tired old man, with not much on his boney hips but his dull skin.

Scardio was left in a small field, in the hot sun with no shelter. He wasn't fed often and his water trough was dirty with flies.

One day as Scardio dozed in the unbearable heat of the day, he heard his mother's voice once more..."keep your head up and ears pricked." As he did this one more time he opened his tired eyes and saw a young boy near the gate to his paddock.

The young boys name was Zaen, and he had travelled from the little Island of Gili Meno on his fishing boat to fetch horse food for the Island.

Zaen placed a hand gently on Scardio's forehead and began to whisper into his cheek. He blew softly into his nostril, and then emptied his pocket of corn, which Scardio quickly gobbled up.

As Zaen started to walk away, Scardio watched with a heavy heart as the young boy climbed through the broken fencing of the paddock and disappeared.

What Scardio didn't know was that Zaen had made a promise to himself that he would would rescue the old grey horse and bring him back to Gili Meno to live.

However, Scardio's owner had other plans. He was a mean and lazy man and didn't care much for his horses.

He would tell Zaen to spend his money more wisely on a better and younger horse, but Zaen would not listen, for he knew the beauty and character in Scardio was still alive and he just needed to feel loved once more.

On Zaen's 7th visit, he noticed Scardio had caught himself on the broken fencing in his paddock and had hurt his leg very badly, but the lazy owner refused to buy Scardio the medicine that he needed.

Zaen fell to his knees, begging the owner to release Scardio, and, that day, the owner finally gave in to the request.

Zaen had built a ramp for Scardio to climb aboard his fishing boat.

Scardio was weak as he stumbled through the sand, dragging his injured leg to where the boat was moored. Scardio put all his trust in Zaen, who skippered the boat back to Gili Meno as carefully and quickly as he could.

The pair arrived just as the sun was going down. Zaen already had a stable ready and slept with the old horse until morning, keeping a watchful eye over Scardio, taking water and feed to where he lay.

When the sun came up, Zaen cleaned Scardio's injured leg and encouraged Scardio to stand. Word soon got out amongst the other horses in Zaen's care and they stood around the pair, telling stories of all the wonderful trips they took around the island with visitors.

Scardio listened intently, realising that he had something in common with each and every one of these horses. They had all been rescued from Lombok by Zaen and now they had a wonderful life showing the very beautiful Island of Gili Meno to tourists who came from all around the world.

It wasn't long before Scardio was feeling better. All the good food had made him stronger and his leg only had a scar to remind him of this old life.

Zaen put on scardio's bridle, climbed up onto the tall grey horse, they walked steadily towards the beach.

Scardio had never seen water so clear and felt sand so soft. They played in the water for hours and the old grey stallion felt alive and so happy to be allowed to live out his days with his new friend Zaen.

ND - #0013 - 271020 - C24 - 210/210/2 - PB - 9781784566234 - Gloss Lamination